Shubh Diwali!

Chitra Soundar

illustrated by **Charlene Chua**

Albert Whitman & Company
Chicago, Illinois

Grandpa watches the waning moon.
The festival is coming soon.

Our house must
look its very best.

Diwali's here,
no time to rest.

We hang buntings of
mango leaves.
They welcome gods,
Grandma believes.

Rangoli art dispels the gloom.
It brings sparkle to every room.

We wear new clothes
to mark the cheer.
We have waited,
all through the year.

Time for stories
about our gods.

Who fought evil
against all odds.

We ring the bells
this darkest night.

We sing the hymns,
chant and recite.

The moon is new,
as night descends.

We light the lamps,
with all our friends.

We exchange gifts and homemade sweets.

We greet our neighbors
on the streets.

Fireworks
whiz, shimmer,
and glow.

The skies brighten in the sparkly show.

Dinner's ready; it's full of treats.

We stay awake, as night retreats.

It's good fortune, the New Year brings.
It's lucky to start brand-new things.

Shubh Diwali,
to one and all.

We wish you joy,
big and small!

Author's Note

Diwali is a festival celebrated across five days by Hindus around the world. Those who come from the North of India celebrate Diwali on the night of the new moon, which is also considered the birth anniversary of the goddess of wealth, Lakshmi. This is the darkest night of fall and marks the transition from the monsoon season and autumn to winter.

As the festival approaches, people tidy their homes and decorate with buntings made of mango leaves and strings of flowers. Homes are also decorated with rangoli—designs and patterns of stars, lamps, and flowers made from rice flour and colored powders.

On the second night of the festival, grown-ups and children dress in new clothes. After lighting lamps and ringing bells to welcome the gods, elders lead prayers and hymns. The day after the new moon's night is celebrated as the mark of a new year. Elders retell stories from the Hindu epics that show us that good always triumphs over evil. On this third day, people give thanks for their good fortune and offer food and support to those less privileged than themselves. People send greeting cards, exchange boxes of sweets, and join with neighbors from all faiths to light fireworks. Families also gather together for a festive feast.

The fifth day, called Bhai Dooj, is special for brothers and sisters, who get together and celebrate their love for one another.

Hindus in the South of India, like me, celebrate Diwali on the second day of the festival to mark the victory of good over evil. Sikhs mark this day as Bandi Chhor Divas to celebrate the release of their leader, Guru Hargobind, who was imprisoned by the Mughal emperor Jahangir. People of other faiths, such as Jainism and Buddhism, also mark Diwali with celebrations.

Growing up in the South of India, I looked forward all year to celebrating Diwali. On the second morning of the festival, as we prepared for the ceremonial oil bath, my grandmother told stories. I loved putting on my new silk skirt and blouse, lighting sparklers, and arranging lamps around the house. Diwali is one of my favorite festivals, and I celebrate it wherever I live.

Shubh Diwali to you!

The Five Days of Diwali

Day 1: Dhan Theras or Dhanvantari Trayodashi
The official beginning of the festival. This day marks when Lord Dhanvantari gave the Ayurveda medical science to humans.

Day 2: Naraka Chaturdasi
The second day marks when Lord Krishna vanquished the demon Naraka to rescue 16,000 princesses he held captive. Hindus in the South of India hold their main celebration on this day to commemorate the victory of good over evil.

Day 3: Day of Diwali
New Year's Day is celebrated, and it marks the birth of Lakshmi, the goddess of wealth.

Day 4: Day of Govardana Puja
This day commemorates when Lord Krishna saved the village of Vrindavan from torrential rains by lifting up a mountain. Prayers are performed, offering a feast to Mother Nature to celebrate the bounties of trees, mountains, and other natural resources.

Day 5: Bhai Dooj
The last day of the festival marks when Krishna returned home to his sister Subhadra after defeating the demon Naraka. Today brothers visit their sisters and celebrate their love for each other.

Glossary

rangoli (rang-oʊ-li)—Traditional floor decorations and patterns made from rice flour and colored powders

Shubh (sh-ʊ-b)—Auspicious or holy

Diwali (Di-wɔ-li)—Another name for the festival of Deepavali, which means 'an array of lamps'

To friends and family, near and afar—CS

For all who light the way through darkness—CC

Library of Congress Cataloging-in-Publication data is on file with the publisher.

Text copyright © 2019 by Chitra Soundar
Illustrations copyright © 2019 by Charlene Chua
First published in the United States of America in 2019 by Albert Whitman & Company
ISBN 978-0-8075-7355-6 (hardcover)
ISBN 978-0-8075-7356-3 (ebook)

Printed in China
10 9 8 7 6 5 4 3 2 1 WKT 24 23 22 21 20 19

Design by Aphee Messer

For more information about Albert Whitman & Company,
visit our website at www.albertwhitman.com.

100 years of Albert Whitman & Company
Celebrate with us in 2019!